A NOTE TO PARENTS

Disney's First Readers Level 1 books were developed with the beginning reader in mind. They feature large, easy-to-read type, lots of repetition, and simple vocabulary.

One of the most important ways parents can help their child develop a love of reading is by providing an *environment* for reading. Every time you discuss a book, read aloud to your child, or your child observes you reading, you promote the development of early reading skills and habits. Here are some tips to help you use **Disney's First Readers Level 1** books with your child:

★ Tell the story about the original Disney film or video. Storytelling is crucial to language development. A young child needs a language *foundation* before reading skills can begin to emerge.

★ Talk about the illustrations in the book. Beginning readers need to use illustrations to gather clues about unknown words or to understand the story.

★ Read aloud to your child. When you read aloud, run your finger smoothly under the text. Do not stop at each word. Enliven the text for your child by using a different voice for each character. In other words, be an actor—and have fun!

★ "Read it again!" Children love hearing stories read again and again. When they begin reading on their own, repetition helps them feel successful. Maintain patience, be encouraging, and expect to read the same books over and over.

★ Play "question and answer." Use the After-Reading Fun activities provided at the end of each book to further enhance your child's learning process.

Remember that early-reading experiences that you share with your child can help him or her to become a confident and successful reader later on!

— Patricia Koppman
Past President
International Reading Association

First published by Disney Press, New York, New York.
This edition published by Scholastic Inc.,
90 Old Sherman Turnpike, Danbury, Connecticut 06816
by arrangement with Disney Licensed Publishing.

SCHOLASTIC and associated logos are trademarks
and/or registered trademarks of Scholastic Inc.

ISBN 0-7172-6680-X

Printed in the U.S.A.

Disney's
Cinderella
Run, Gus, Run!

by Patrick Daley
Illustrated by Sol Studios

Disney's First Readers — Level 1
A Story from Disney's *Cinderella*

SCHOLASTIC INC.
New York   Toronto   London   Auckland   Sydney
Mexico City   New Delhi   Hong Kong   Buenos Aires

It is time
for a party.

It is time for some fun.

There will be lots of treats.

So tell everyone.

Tell all the birds.

Tell Bruno, too.

There is just one
you should not tell.

Yes, you know who.
You know very well.

Run, Gus, run!
It is Lucifer the cat.

Run, Gus, run!
Run from that cat.

Do not let him catch you.
Run faster than that!

Climb up the table.

Hop over the bowl.

Dive under the bag.

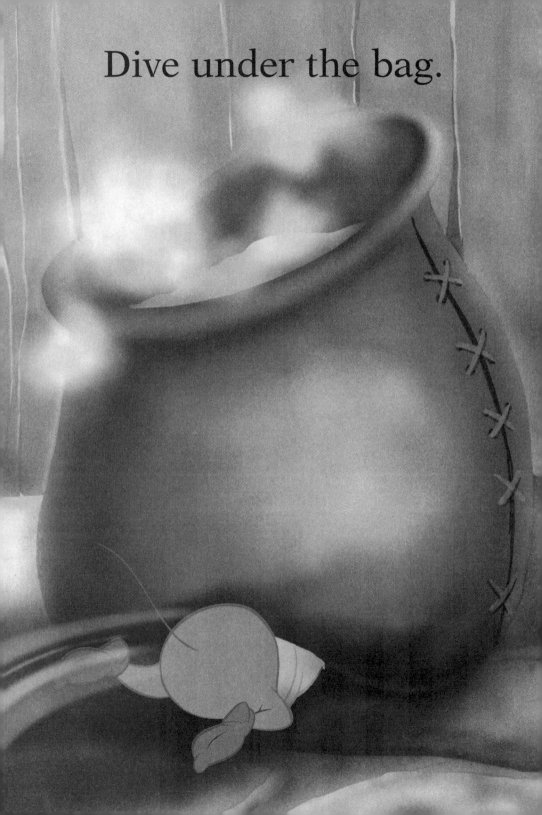

Jump through the hole.

Run, Gus, run!
Run from that cat.

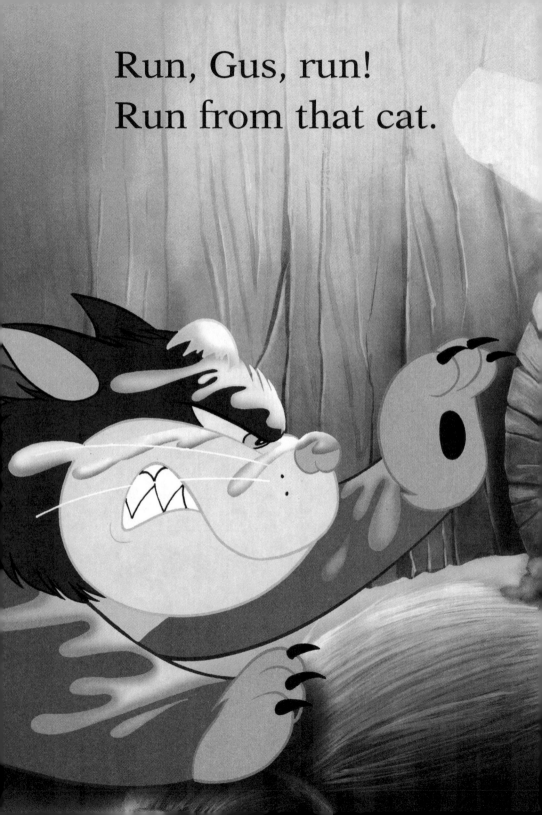

Do not let him catch you.
Run faster than that!

Now Gus is in trouble.
What can he do?

Tell Cinderella.
She will help you.

It is time for the party.
It is time for some fun.
Everyone is happy.
(Well, almost everyone!)

AFTER-READING FUN

Enhance the reading experience with follow-up questions to help your child develop reading comprehension and increase his/her awareness of words.

Approach this with a sense of play. Make a game of having your child answer the questions. You do not need to ask all the questions at one time. Let these questions be fun discussions rather than a test. If your child doesn't have instant recall, encourage him/her to look back into the book to "research" the answers. You'll be modeling what good readers do and, at the same time, forging a sharing bond with your child.

Run, Gus, Run!

1. Who did Gus tell about the party?

2. Who should *not* have been told about the party?

3. Who rescued Gus?

4. Why was Lucifer unhappy?

5. What kind of party did they have?

6. What do you like to do on your birthday?